The
Blue Door

Published in Canada by Fitzhenry & Whiteside,
195 Allstate Parkway, Markham, Ontario L3R 4T8

Published in the United States by Fitzhenry & Whiteside,
121 Harvard Avenue, Suite 2, Allston, Massachusetts 02134

Printed in Hong Kong

10 9 8 7 6 5 4 3 2 1

National Library of Canada Cataloguing in Publication Data

McPhail, David, 1940-
The blue door : a fox and rabbit story

ISBN 1-55041-647-2

I. O'Connor, John, 1947-   II. Title.

PZ7.M24B1 2001   j813'.54   C2001-901077-X

U.S. Cataloging-in-Publication Data
(Library of Congress Standards)

McPhail, David.
The blue door : a fox and rabbit story / by David McPhail ; illustrated by John O'Connor.—1st ed.
[32] p. : col. ill. ; cm.
Summary: A case of mistaken identity leads to hilarious results when fox and rabbit set out to visit an uncle in the city.
IBSN 1-55041-6472
1. City — Fiction. 2. Friends — Fiction. I. O'Connor, John. II. Title.
[E] 21 2001 AC CIP

Fitzhenry & Whiteside acknowledges with thanks the Canada Council for the Arts, the Government of Canada through the Book Publishing Industry Development Program (BPIDP), and the Ontario Arts Council for their support of our publishing program.

Design by Wycliffe Smith

The
Blue Door

A Fox and Rabbit Story
By David McPhail

Illustrated
by John O'Connor

Fitzhenry & Whiteside

In memory of my brother
Brian O'Connor
who was loved by children, dogs, cats
and surely by foxes and rabbits too
–John

For John O'Connor,
artist and friend
–David

Fox was in a hurry.
He ran to Rabbit's house.

"Where are you going, Fox?"
asked Rabbit.

"I'm going to the city to visit my uncle,"
replied Fox. "I haven't seen him
since I was a pup."

"Have a good time," said Rabbit.
"I will miss you."

"No, you won't," said Fox.
"You are coming with me."

"I am?" said Rabbit. "Is it all right
with your uncle?"

Fox nodded. "Oh, he will be pleased
that I've brought along a friend.
You will like him. Uncle tells the most
interesting stories."

"Oh, I love stories," said Rabbit.
And he packed his bag.

"What does your uncle look like?"
said Rabbit as they walked to the city.

Fox replied, "Well, I can't quite remember
what he looks like. But I do remember
his stories and I know where he lives."

"Do you have his address?"
said Rabbit.

Fox shook his head.
"Well, not exactly. But I do
remember that his house
has a blue door."

"That is sure to be helpful,"
said Rabbit.

The two friends walked all day.
They walked until they were tired.

Finally they reached the city.

"I don't remember it being this big,"
said Fox.

"But all we have to do
is find a blue door."

So they walked up one street
and down another.

Suddenly Fox stopped.

"There's the blue door!" he cried.

Fox knocked on the door.
Slowly the door opened, and there stood
a stout old badger.

"Who is it?" the badger asked.
"I seem to have lost my glasses, and I can't see
very well without them."

"It's me, Uncle," said Fox cheerily.
"Your long-lost nephew!"

"Well, well, well," said the badger.
And he gave Fox a big hug.

"Welcome. Come in and have some tea.
Make yourself at home."

"This is my friend, Rabbit," Fox told the badger.

"Then he must have tea
as well," the badger
said.

As they drank their tea,
Fox said, "Uncle, I still remember
your interesting
stories."

So Fox told the story of the runaway apple cart that bumped into the pie wagon.

Then he told the story of the pumpkin
that rolled down the hill and landed
on top of the statue
in the square.

"Uncle," said Fox, " tell Rabbit about the time the whale swallowed your fishing boat. I remember that story was my favorite."

"But...I never had a boat," said the badger. "I don't recall any such story."

"Oh, dear," said Fox. "All I can remember is Uncle's blue door."